I CAN AND I WILL! I AM THE GREATEST! I BELIEVE IN ME! I AM BRAVE! I AM STRONG!

This book belongs to

SO-CFR-432

I HAVE MANY GIFTS AND TALENTS! I AM KIND! I AM HELPFUL! I DO MY BEST IN WORK AND TASKS! I AM A TEAM PLAYER! I AM LOVED!

To my little loves, Billy and Luke, for being two of the bravest people I know and teaching me a thing or two about courage. May you always remember the magic words and take them with you wherever you go, because you can overcome anything and be anything as long as you **BELIEVE**. I believe in you and love you more than you know.

www.mascotbooks.com

Biddy Squiddy's Magic Words

For more information, please contact:
Mascot Books
620 Herndon Parkway #320
Herndon, VA 20170
info@mascotbooks.com

Library of Congress Control Number: 2019900608

CPSIA Code: PRT0319A
ISBN-13: 978-1-64307-446-7

Printed in the United States

BIDDY SQUIDDY'S
MAGIC WORDS

I AM BRAVE AND I CAN CONQUER ANY WAVE

Written by Tracie Main
Illustrations by Justo Borrero

It was a day like every other, except this day Biddy Squiddy got a request from his mother.

"It's time for you to brave the wide open sea and catch dinner for the family."

Biddy Squiddy was not pleased and replied, "Who me? The littlest squid? I'll be caught and fried! What about Biggy Squiddy? He's much bigger than me."

"No, Biddy Squiddy," replied his mommy. "It's time for you to learn the ways of the sea. You're old enough now, grab your things and flee."

Biddy Squiddy didn't like this idea at all, so he protested, "I'm much too small. Plus, there's something wrong with my ink. It doesn't work right, I must have a kink."

But Biddy Squiddy's mommy didn't worry and shooed him out in a hurry. Just before he swam away, she said, "Wait, I have something important to say."

She wrapped him in a hug, held him close and snug. And then she said, "When you're scared say these words and you'll find courage instead: I am brave and can conquer any wave!"

Then, she handed him a pen and said, "Use this if you must. It's full of magic ink that you can trust."

Biddy Squiddy was so scared, but he knew he had to go. So he left the comfort of his coral reef and went along with the flow. The sea carried him and his magic pen and he wondered if he'd ever see his mommy again.

Shark Park, Seal Sandbar, and Seahorse Harbor were where he'd have to swim through. How he'd make it through them all, he hadn't a clue.

As he approached Shark Park, he felt his ink get weak.
The sharks were all out playing a game of Hide-N-Seek.
But Biddy Squiddy knew he had to get to the other side.
So he weighed his options and decided to play along
and hide.

Unfortunately, the biggest shark of them all spotted him, opened his mouth, and said, "Jump in!"

Biddy Squiddy shook with fear, and held his magic pen near. Then suddenly, he remembered what his mom said, and shouted the words and found courage instead. "I am brave and can conquer any wave!"

And wouldn't you know, the magic pen did a fancy dance and burst out an ink rainbow. Into the shark's mouth it went, and sealed it shut just like cement.

Biddy Squiddy couldn't believe his eyes and was overjoyed to escape Shark Park alive.

As Biddy Squiddy swam along, the sun peered in strong. All of this could only mean one thing; Seal Sandbar was close and nearing.

Just then, a silver seal torpedoed past him and sent him flying into quite the spin. All of this made him feel seasick and when he came to, he was face to face with the seal now too.

"It's my lucky day," cheered the silver seal as he scooped up Biddy Squiddy for a meal.

Biddy Squiddy shook with fear and held his magic pen near. Then suddenly, he remembered what his mom said, and shouted the words and found courage instead. "I am brave and can conquer any wave!"

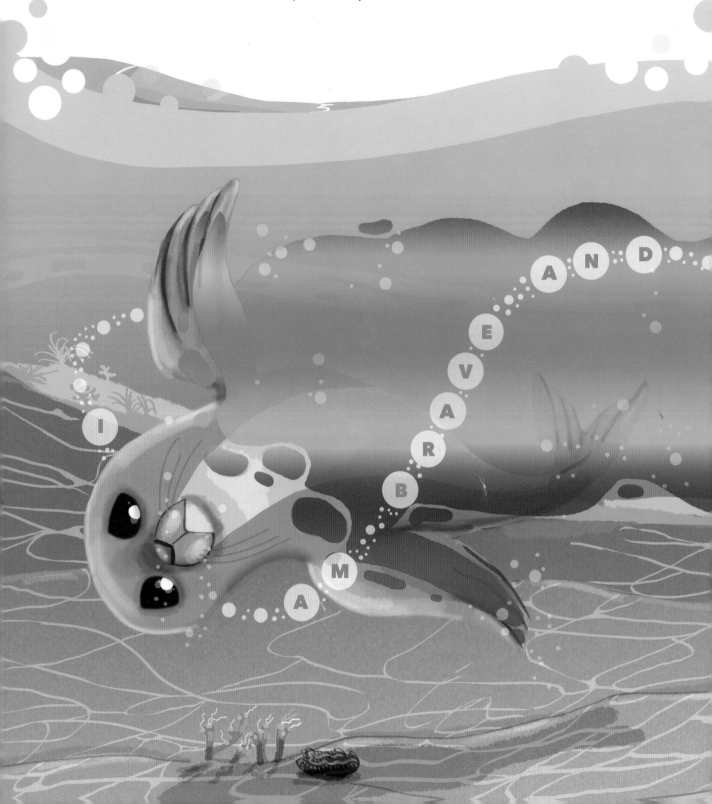

And wouldn't you know, the magic pen did a fancy dance and burst out an ink rainbow. Into the silver seal's flippers it went, and Biddy Squiddy popped free from this frightful event.

Biddy Squiddy was so surprised and was overjoyed to escape Seal Sandbar alive.

Biddy Squiddy's dinner assignment was almost complete. He could finally see the market down on Ocean Street! But as he got closer an anchor soared down and one by one, the hooks came all around.

Biddy Squiddy froze with fear and suddenly, he got hooked out of nowhere. The hook yanked him straight up to the top of the ocean where the fishermen and boats were causing a commotion. But then suddenly, he remembered what his mom said, and shouted the words and found courage instead. "I am brave and can conquer any wave!"

And wouldn't you know, the magic pen did a fancy dance and burst out an ink rainbow. Into the seahorse hooks it went and helped him unsnag and zig-zag safely to the market tent.

Biddy Squiddy felt twice his size and was overjoyed to escape Seahorse Harbor alive.

Finally, he arrived at the market and grabbed some fresh kelp from the shelf. He couldn't believe he was actually shopping all by himself.

On the way home, Biddy Squiddy passed by all of the places he had feared. But this time all the predators waved and cheered.

When he returned home, Biddy Squiddy's mommy was so proud and the whole family gathered around. It was dinnertime and they sat to eat. Biddy Squiddy had accomplished quite a feat!

That night, Biddy Squiddy's mommy tucked him into bed. "There's no magic ink in this pen," she said. "It's the magic in the words that got you through, but more importantly it's because you believed in you."

Biddy Squiddy went to bed feeling brave and knew he could conquer any wave.

Did you know?
Squid can squirt ink when they are feeling scared near a predator. The ink forms a cloud and allows the squid to hide and escape.

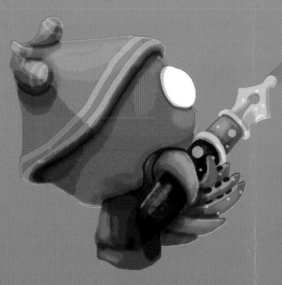

ABOUT THE AUTHOR

Tracie Main attended the University of Iowa as a theatre arts major, then moved to Los Angeles where she landed several roles in television and became an active member of the SAG Union. Tracie has always been a writer at heart and has written many published and unpublished works. Her keen understanding of character development as an actress contributed to the successful creation of her children's books. She was taught at a young age by her father, beauty industry leader and educator John Amico, about the power of self-belief. Her passion is teaching children to believe in themselves and that they're capable of accomplishing great things. She currently resides in Chicago with her husband and two young boys. Tracie is available to conduct workshops for your school, library, or event.

Visit **www.traciemain.com** to book an author visit or workshop.

ALSO AVAILABLE

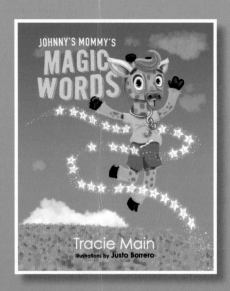

JOHNNY'S MOMMY'S MAGIC WORDS

"I can and I will & I am the greatest!"

Helping build confidence and
self-belief in kids!